Big Brother Dustin

Alden R. Carter

Photographs by **Dan Young** *with* **Carol Carter**

Albert Whitman & Company · Morton Grove, Illinois

ABOUT THE AUTHOR AND PHOTOGRAPHERS

Alden R. Carter is the author of thirty books for children and young adults, including the celebrated novels *Dogwolf, Up Country,* and *Between a Rock and a Hard Place.* With his daughter, Siri, he wrote *I'm Tougher Than Asthma!,* an American Bookseller "Pick of the List" for 1995. He lives in Marshfield, Wisconsin.

Dan Young is the award-winning photojournalist of the *Marshfield News Herald.* His work has appeared in the *Washington Post,* the *Milwaukee Journal, Current Science,* and numerous other newspapers and magazines, as well as internationally through the Associated Press. In 1995, he was awarded Best of Show by the Wisconsin News Photographers Association. This is his second collaboration with Mr. Carter.

Carol S. Carter is a graduate of the Rocky Mountain School of Photography in Missoula, Montana. Her photographs have appeared in two previous books by her husband, Alden: *Modern China* and *The Battle of Gettysburg.*

The book shown on p. 8 is *You Were Born on Your Very First Birthday (text copyright © 1983 by Linda Walvoord Girard; illustrations copyright © 1983 by Christa Kieffer; published in 1983 by Albert Whitman & Company).*

Text copyright © 1997 by Alden R. Carter.
Photographs copyright © 1997 by Dan Young.
Published in 1997 by Albert Whitman & Company,
6340 Oakton Street, Morton Grove, Illinois 60053-2723.
Published simultaneously in Canada
by General Publishing, Limited, Toronto.
Printed in the United States of America.
10 9 8 7 6 5 4 3 2

The design is by Karen A. Yops.
The text typeface is Stone Informal.

Library of Congress Cataloging-in-Publication Data

Carter, Alden R.
  Big brother Dustin / written by Alden Carter; photographs by Dan Young and Carol Carter.
     p.   cm.
  Summary: A boy with Down syndrome helps his parents and grandparents get ready for the birth of his baby sister and chooses the perfect name for her.
  ISBN 0-8075-0715-6
  [1. Brothers and sisters—Fiction. 2. Babies—Fiction. 3. Down syndrome—Fiction. 4. Mentally handicapped—Fiction.] I. Young, Dan, photographer, ill. II. Carter, Carol S., ill. III. Title.
PZ7.C2426Bi   1997
[E]—dc20   96-27301
                                                           CIP
                                                           AC

For Dustin Apfel and Chelsea Akin

Many thanks to all who helped with *Big Brother Dustin,* particularly John, Janet, Katie, and Steven Apfel; Dan, Judy, and Jacob Akin; Roger and Bea Pittsley; June and Myron Haglund; Susan and Anna Rose Durst; Cathy Sutterer; Robin Safford; Mindy Gribble; and Ruthie Watt. Our families and our editor, Abby Levine, have our special gratitude.

One summer day, Dustin's mom and dad brought home wonderful news. "We're going to have a baby girl," Dustin's mom said.

"You're going to be a big brother, champ," his dad said.

Nana Olson started crying.

"Don't worry, Dustin," said Papa Olson. "She's just real happy."

To celebrate, they went out for pizza. When they got home, Dad called his parents in Minneapolis.

"Is Grandma Strohman crying?" Dustin asked.

"No," Dad said. "But I think Grandpa might. Here, you tell him."

The next morning, Dustin told the whole world the big news:
"We're going to have a baby!"

Dustin's mom said gently, "Don't get too excited just yet. We have to wait months and months for your baby sister to get here." She explained how the baby would grow inside her until she was big enough and strong enough to be born.

"When will that be?" Dustin asked.

"Just after New Year's, when it's very cold."

"Brrr," said Dustin. "We'll have to keep her warm."

In the fall, they started getting the baby's room ready.
Dustin helped set up the crib he'd used when he was a baby.
"What's our baby's name going to be?" he asked.
"I don't know," his dad said. "Your mom and I can't think
of the right one. Maybe you can think of the perfect name."

Dustin thought hard all day. He liked lots of names, but he especially liked Ann, Grandma Strohman's name, and Mary, Nana Olson's name. But Nana made a face when he asked her if they should name the baby Mary. "That's a nice idea, Dustin, but your other nana might be sad if we used my name and not hers."

Dustin helped his mom get out the baby clothes and blankets. "We could name her Laura, like you," Dustin said.

"No," his mom said. "Then people would always be getting us mixed up."

"Maybe we should name her Honeybun," Dustin said. "I heard Daddy call you that." But Dustin's mom made a face, and he knew that Honeybun wasn't the perfect name, either.

Dustin and his dad put a mobile over the crib so the baby would have something to watch. "Maybe we should call her AnnMary," Dustin said. But his dad made a face, and Dustin knew that AnnMary wasn't quite right, either.

After Thanksgiving, Dustin's mom took him to a class at the hospital to learn how to be a big brother. They peeked into the nursery.

"Do all these babies have names?" Dustin asked.
"Every one," his mom said.

A nurse taught the children how to diaper their favorite dolls and stuffed animals. "Now you'll be able to show your mom and dad if they forget how to change the baby," she said.

The girl across from Dustin said, "We're going to call our baby Nathan if he's a boy and Rachel if she's a girl. My name's Barbara Ann."

Dustin, who was busy diapering his doll Charlie, said, "I like the Ann part. That's my grandma's name."

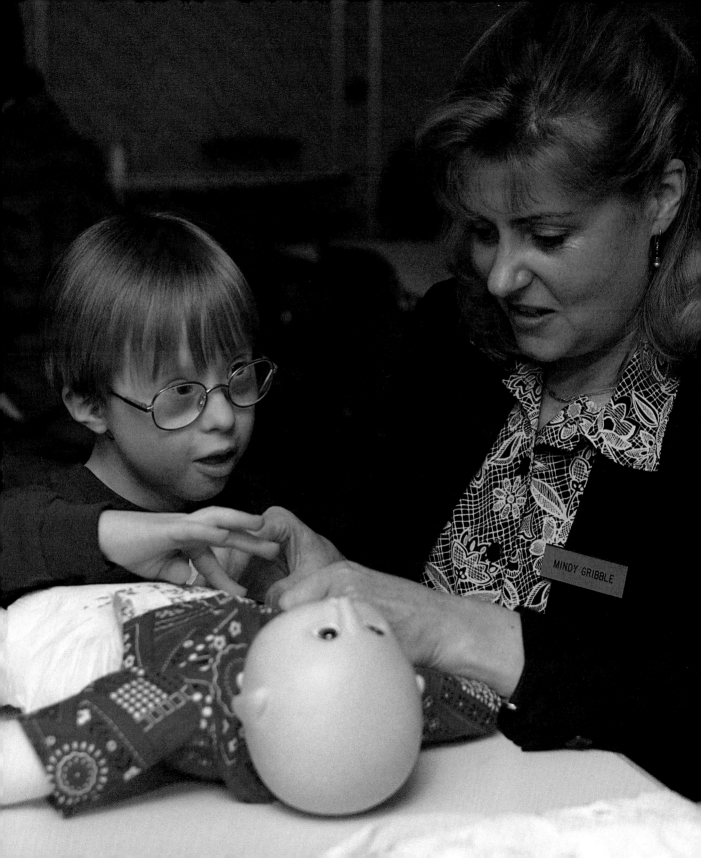

It was almost New Year's. Dustin's mom had another doctor's appointment, and Dustin had to sit a long time in the waiting room. He'd thought about a lot of names. Mary. Ann. Laura. Honeybun. AnnMary. Barbara Ann. Maybe he'd ask his dad what *he* thought of naming the baby Honeybun.

Waiting was hard on everyone now.

"Don't worry, Dad," Dustin said. "MaryAnn won't make us wait forever."

"What did you call her?" Dustin's dad asked.

"MaryAnn. Hey, that sounds pretty good!"

"You bet it does," said his dad. "Laura," he called. "Dustin thought of the perfect name!"

A few days later, Dustin woke up to hear Nana Olson singing in the kitchen. He rushed downstairs. "What's going on?" he asked.

"The baby came in the night. Your mom and dad are at the hospital now," Nana said.

"Let's go!" Dustin yelled.

Nana made Dustin eat breakfast before they left. At the hospital gift shop, Dustin bought a balloon for MaryAnn and flowers for his mom. "I bet Mom would like a pizza, too," he said. "Maybe tomorrow," said Nana.

At the door to the hospital room, Dustin hung back, just a tiny bit afraid. But only for a moment.

"There's our boy," Dustin's dad called. "Come on in, champ."

"Dustin, meet MaryAnn," his mom said. "MaryAnn, this is Dustin."

"Hi, MaryAnn," said Dustin. "I'm your big brother."

And though she was very little and very sleepy, he thought she smiled.

Here's MaryAnn!

Swing-a-bye, baby!

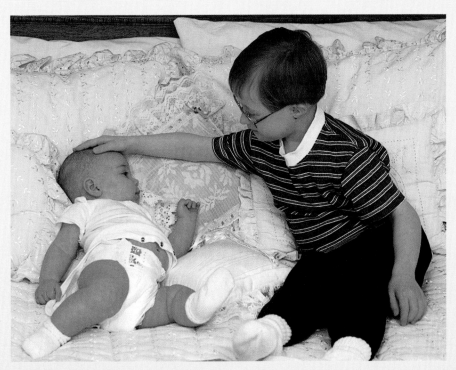

Fuzzy-wuzzy
is MaryAnn.

Time for lunch.

"What's my big brother got now?"

"I want the motorcycle!"

"Mom, you do it <u>this</u> way."

"See, MaryAnn, standing isn't so tough!"

"Giddyap,
Dad!"

It's raining!

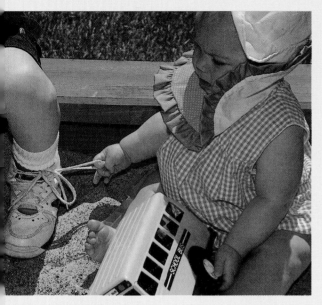

One, two, untie the shoe.

"Uh-uh, too small for baby!"

Pop the bubbles, MaryAnn.

"See you later, alligator!"